I0518700

The Erotic Robot

Anne Palace

Contents

Are You Spoiled or Lonely?

M arch 23, 2031

I've decided to keep a diary. I don't know why. I never have before. The idea came to me today when I was sitting at Les Deux Maggot café near the Saint German des Pres metro. I went to visit my best friend Kira, who lives on Rue Bonaparte in a lovely one bedroom on the second floor. I stopped at the Eglise Saint German des Pres, it finally got renovated a couple of years ago, so I wanted to see if it was as beautiful as Kira claimed, then I had the sudden urge to sit at the Deux Maggots. I hadn't been there for a long time and wanted an over-priced café crème and some time to think. About what? About life, about my past, my future, to write it all down. I'm not a writer, but why not? What can it hurt to jot down some stuff to clear my head?

I picked a table on the boulevard and started writing. I watched men, women stroll down the boulevard and with each sip I would follow their lives, and pretend I knew them personally, as if knew their thoughts and feelings, like I am some omnipresent God, who can read their minds. I

can know their plans, thoughts, lives, happiness, pain, and disappoint-
ments.

You can't really get into anyone's head, but it's an exercise. What if I
could get in their heads? Know what makes them tick? What motivates
them? Why do they like what they like? Hate what they hate? Love who
they love?

Look at my jumbled mess. Ha! Ha! Told you (who is you?), I'm not a
writer.

Today is kind of a cloudy day in Paris, but not too cold. I still had to
put on a leather jacket and wrap my scarf around my neck to keep the
cold out. I think I look good, at least not too old, and I look chic. My hair
looks nice. Men still turn their heads and flirt with me. Sometimes, I
flirt back when they look nice.

Right this moment, I have a buzzing in my head and a longing in
my heart for something, but I'm not sure for what. My thoughts are
all jumbled in my mind. I don't know where to start making sense of
myself.

Even Kira said, "Belen, you seem distracted. What's going on?"

"Am I?" I answered as we sat on her plush sofa purchased at the
Galleries Lafayette. I was there purchasing this over-priced sofa with
her.

I stroked the fur on her Persian cat, which jumped in my lap as soon
as I sat down. The sun shone brightly through her half-closed, French
windows intermittently, but it was only the end of March, and the
weather outside in Paris was still chilly and the skies were, sometimes,
cloudy threatening a drizzle, or even a rain out.

"You should start dating again. You know, see what's out there," she
says.

I felt my eyes start to roll at the idea, then stopped myself. "I've been dating. Remember what happened with that guy that I went out with a couple of months ago?"

"Who, Bernard?"

"Yes, that one, the professor guy," I answered. It was another bad memory in the repertoire of bad memories I'd had in the last few years with relationships, each one having ended with a bad feeling in my heart and a sour taste in my mouth.

Kira sighed. "Yeah, that didn't go so well. Pretty disappointing. Have you heard anything about Miles?"

I felt a stab of pain and anger flash in my chest. "No, why would I hear anything about Miles? It's been two years since I talked to him. Remember, he went back to London with his girlfriend."

"More wine?" She poured herself another full glass. Was she planning to get drunk on a Saturday afternoon?

I nodded a 'no.' "Let's not talk about Miles again. Not today, not ever." I stroked the Persian a little more vigorously and it purred softly in my lap.

Kira started sipping quickly, "You're too young to give up."

"I hate French men," I answered, looking at the cat.

Kira smiled a little. "You were married to an Englishman, and you hate only Frenchmen?"

"I wish I had been married to no one. Thank God we didn't have kids."

Kira nodded. "Do you regret it really?"

"No," I said and smiled a little. "I really don't. Everything in life is a lesson or at least I'd like to believe that." I sighed. "That doesn't change the fact that I'm a 37 year old divorcee."

"So, what?" answered Kira. "I'm already 34. You don't see me dying because I'm not married yet."

"You have Paul," I said. "He's a descent guy."

"Yeah, Paul. He's good. I suppose. He doesn't seem to be dying to propose."

I crossed my legs again and stared at Kira's picture of the Eiffel tower on the wall. "You say you're not dying to get married."

"I don't know what I'm dying to do. I suppose if I don't get married soon, then I won't pop out a baby ever." Kira stared at me with her dark eyes and perfect, red lip stick lips. I wondered why Paul wouldn't want to marry her. Men are strange like that.

"Do you want to "pop" one out, as you say?" I laughed.

Kira looked at me seriously. "Somehow, sometimes I feel if I don't, that I'll regret it one day."

I didn't reply right away thinking about what she said. "That's just society telling you that if you're female you have to be a mother before it's too late, you have to get married before it's too late. You have a shelf life like some sort of gourmet, takeout dinner. If you don't get picked up and eaten by a certain date, then you're no longer edible, but, if you do all of those things, you'll be happy, and live happily ever after like in a fairy tale, but, if the fairy tale doesn't work out..." I paused, not sure if I should set myself up as the example of a failed fairytale princess. "...you'll end up divorced like me or possibly with a kid, and divorced."

"I suppose anything is possible," Kira said. "I just don't want to be an inedible gourmet dinner. She laughed slightly. "So, what do you suggest I do?"

"With Paul? Or about marriage and motherhood?"

Kira laughed. "All of them."

"I have no idea. It's not for me to say anything about Paul and I'm a failure in the last two."

"Don't be hard on yourself like that. I hate it when you do that. You'll find happiness one day. You just haven't found the right one."

Kira is a good friend. She'd always been there for me and supported my choices. We've known each other since our university days. She is my closest friend and I think that I've told her almost everything about myself. No one tells everyone everything. We all have hidden things within ourselves that we want no one to know. No one knows our thoughts, our true feelings, or our deepest desires, or our deepest regrets.

"Love is right around the corner. You never know." I laughed. "I'd better be going. I have some stuff to do before Monday." It was a Saturday afternoon.

We both got up and Kira walked me to the door. "Salut, A bientôt." She gave me a kiss on the cheek as is our custom.

The conversation went something like this, then I was on the street walking toward the église and the Les Deux Maggots.

Belen was born lucky. She had the benefit of being born to a French father and a Spanish mother. They met in Spain and moved to Paris, had Belen, and lived together until her mother passed away right after Belen finished university. Her father still lives on the outskirts of Paris in a three-bedroom house, which he purchased for the family, after he did well for himself in sales for about five years. Belen's brother, Pierre, was born a few years later and still lives in the house with their father, while saving up to buy an apartment in the center of Paris, so that he can live, and work close to his job.

Belen's mother inherited a small fortune of 200,000 euros from her father from his apartment sale in Madrid after his death, plus an apartment in the 5th arrondisement of Paris, and when she died she left Belen one-third of the money and the apartment.

Belen's parents had a good and average life together until Belen's mother died. Whether they had true love or real passion together is debatable, but neither one had a serious discussion of separating and since they seemed to get along fairly well, except for when her father would lash out at her mother for stupid, little things, and they had arguments, but stayed married.

After university, Belen started her finance career by going to London to work at a large bank, where she met Miles, who worked at the same place. After dating for a year, they got married and moved back to Paris, where Belen opened her own consulting business, while Miles, who didn't know French, and didn't have a job, sat around enjoying the good life in the city of lights.

For some reason, still incomprehensible to Belen, Miles not only lost interest in work, but he also lost interest in Belen, and over the next few years, not only did they no longer have anything in common, but they didn't do anything together, or enjoy each other's company anymore.

Time went by like this until five years passed and until one day Belen had had enough and told Miles that she wanted a divorce, to which Miles, never flinching at that announcement or begging for a second chance, finally, got jolted out of his self-indulgent stupor, packed his belongings, and moved out.

The divorce proceedings took a long time as they usually do in France, but since they didn't have children together and Miles didn't have another woman, the court finally granted the divorce ordering Belen, to pay Miles a small monthly alimony until, as the judge aptly put it, "he gets back on his feet." This was Belen's only regret; that she had to pay him to get out of her life.

Miles wasted no time in finding his manhood and employment again. Also, he found himself a girlfriend. The alimony came to an end and so did the bitterness over the divorce, and the feeling that Belen had that Miles never fought with one ounce of his being for their marriage, and the bitter conclusion that he must have never loved her in the first place. In fact, Belen wasn't sure why Miles married her. Maybe, it was something he felt that he should do.

When she sat at the *Les Deux Maggots* drinking her café crème, she realized that she never experienced true love as she imagined it. She imagined it to be something worth fighting and sacrificing for. She imagined it to be something that had no end, the two people involved never gave up, but always sought to accommodate each other in any circumstance. These thoughts made her a bit sad and tore at her soul, so she tried to put them out of her mind, and to enjoy her coffee, and people watching.

After sitting at the *Les Deux Maggots* for over an hour and jotting her thoughts in her new diary, Belen decided that it was time to go to her own apartment in the 5th arrondissement. As she walked down the boulevard Saint Germain toward the metro stop, she saw an advertisement for the newest model of robot that looked so human one could barely tell it apart from a human being. The ad said *"La Vie avec Chaz"* starting at 15,000 euros for the basic model. There was a 3D video coming out of the ad showing "Chaz" with his chiseled good looks in a suit, then cooking in the kitchen with an apron on, taking out the trash, and walking a dog in Tuileries, and even at a restaurant with a woman enjoying a good conversation. Then, there were screen shots of "Chaz" with different hair colors, eye colors, and skin tones.

She wondered what the basic model could do versus the deluxe model. She snickered to herself at the thought of going on a date with "Chaz," sitting in a restaurant with him having a conversation, while people stared at her with her mechanical boyfriend wondering what she would do with him later that night.

She wrapped her scarf tighter around her neck and zipped up her leather jacket as the wind started blowing cold and the sky got cloudy again.

Was it so far-fetched a thought that people were purchasing robots as not only helpers, but also as social and sexual companions? When she thought about it, even businesses were starting to get a few Chaz models to help with tasks saving a lot on labor. As a businessperson, Belen knew how that worked. First, there were automatic checkouts at grocery stores, so all those jobs went away, then grocery stores where you didn't shop, but ordered on-line, and came to pick up your bag, then there were stores full of Chaz, and one human supervisor. In fact, as she walked and looked at the café's, there were plenty of Chaz serving customers and having brunch with humans, although, they couldn't actually eat and drink. So, they sat at the table talking to their human companions, while the humans ate and drank.

She wondered if it would be economical and comforting to have a Chaz help her out in the office, working beside her regular assistant, Marina. In the evening, she could have Chaz keep her company at her apartment. Even though she had friends, it did get lonely at times in the evenings after work. She could always walk out on the street and sit at a café, and people watch, if she felt really isolated, but it wasn't the same as having someone in the apartment with her.

15,000 euros wasn't an overwhelming amount of money for her. She had plenty in savings since the consulting business was doing well and she could make it up within a few months. Why not? She could go to the robot store near the office Monday afternoon if she took off early and let Marina handle everything for her. She would at least check it out and, make a decision later.

The rest of the weekend went by peacefully. Kira called on Sunday and they chatted for half an hour. Afterward, Belen went out to Rue Muffatard, which was near her place to eat by herself. Again, she noticed that there were quite a few Chaz accompanying their mistresses around and even sitting with them having lunch or pretending to at least.

The Perfect Man (Robot)

March 25, 2031

Marina was pretty friendly this morning. I suppose that she had a good weekend, although, she didn't tell me much about it.

The morning went smoothly at the office. I'm lucky that I have a good space on the Boulevard de Courcelles near Parc Monceau. Sometimes, when the weather is good during the spring months, I'll get my lunch, and sit out on a bench at the park. Sometimes, Marina comes with me and we chat about work, and other stuff like what movies we saw on t.v. or where she went with her husband, and kid over the weekend. Sometimes, it's hard for me to relate to Marina because I don't have kids and I don't have a husband anymore, so I have nothing to add to the conversation. Marina is a good employee, who has been with me a long time, and so it doesn't matter if her and I aren't that close. She does her job and doesn't miss too many days, and doesn't bring her personal problems to the office.

Around 3 pm, I said to Marina that I was cutting out early today. I didn't tell her where I was going. "Okay, Belen," she answered. "I'll close up at 5:30 pm and get those charts done for your client." She didn't ask

*me where I was going. That was another thing I liked about Marina,
she wasn't nosey.*

*I got on the train at the Monceau metro station and went all the
way to Chateau Rouge stop on the Boulevard Barbes, then got off and
walked five minutes to the robot store called "Celine." Each one was
an independent contractor like a cell phone store, under an umbrella
company called "Bot World."*

*The store was rather large and it had to be since these stores have to
keep a lot of models on the floor for customers to see. As soon as I walked
in a saleswoman in a nice suit nodded at me in acknowledgement.*

*I walked around the showroom a little and looked at all the different
models. The less expensive ones were the outdated, older models that
had metallic voices and looked steel, then came the human looking Chaz
models that were the current craze; these were the ones that were working
as waiters, having lunch and dinner, cooking, and working in offices.
These sounded totally human and looked like a "real" man or woman
(they also had female robots).*

*To be honest, I wasn't interested in another female companion in
the office or as a friend at home. I already had girlfriends. What I
wanted was a good-looking guy to flatter me and possibly have a nice
conversation with. At some point, I would feel bold enough to go sit at a
café with my machine boyfriend for lunch or dinner like some of these
other ladies.*

*I had no idea as to the extent of these Chaz models intellectual capa-
bilities. I knew that they were more than a voice recording, but as to how
they interacted on a personal level, I could only imagine. When I did see
them at cafes or restaurants and they served my friends and I, they were
very capable of taking our orders and reacting to our culinary wishes,
but I had no idea how extensive their vocabulary database was to be able*

to converse in a business setting or on various topics, which didn't involve food or grocery takeout.

The other interesting aspect was that they literally all looked the "alike" with no variation other than hair color or eye color: green, black, brown, blond, blue eyes, brown eyes, or dark brown eyes. Their eyes had a kind of metallic glow, for some reason, which didn't look human.

By that time, the sales lady came over subtly and stood at my side. "Bonjour Madame, can I answer any questions for you?"

I felt a little embarrassed at first. "Bonjour. Yes, well, I was wondering how wide of a vocabulary do they have? I mean, can they converse on any topic or are there some limits?"

"Ah, that's a good question. It really depends on the programming that you're buying. If you start with "basic," then it would only be good for basic tasks and conversations, such as: cooking and cleaning in the house, grocery store errands, and waiting tables. If you want the "medium advanced" model, then we are talking at the level of being able to work at a grocery store or at an office as a basic administrative assistant, plus all of the capabilities of the basic model. The "high advanced" model has the greatest capabilities, of course. It can converse on any topic and has access to the global web, plus, can extrapolate topics, and complex responses based on your interests and wishes. It can do all of the tasks of the less advanced models, plus..." She leaned into my ear a little to almost whisper to me. "it is fully functional in any personal capacity that you may want."

I looked at the lady and felt myself blush slightly. "You mean..." I couldn't get the words out.

The seasoned saleswoman looked at me with no embarrassment and said, "Oh, yes, in the bedroom too! It performs very well in that aspect and I think you wouldn't be disappointed."

My eyes widened a bit with surprise. I coughed a little in discomfort. "Well, that is, I suppose, a huge bonus." I finally blurted out.

"I know that some ladies are not accustomed to discussing these things, but the concept is catching on quickly and many ladies want the advanced model. If you can afford it, it's only 25, 000 euro. That's only 10,000 more than the very basic model."

"I see." I still couldn't wrap my mind around "fully functional" concept, but it seemed a little scary and titillating at the same time to think of a mechanical lover that never got tired.

"Oh, I almost forgot to mention. We do have financing, if you qualify." The sales lady suddenly sounded excited as if she was going to take one home tonight herself.

"I won't need financing. But I do have another question. Why do they all look alike?"

"These are mass manufactured and the process of putting the synthetic skin and facial features is pre-set, so the manufacturer cannot easily alter body type or facial features at this time, but they're working on it. Maybe, in another year there will be different features, as well as 'made to order.' Would you like to talk to one?"

"Yes, why not?" I said enthusiastically.

The sales lady walked up to one of the Chaz and reached behind his neck at the hairline. Suddenly, the previously asleep Chaz opened his eyes and picked up his head. He smiled slightly at us. "Bonjour, mesdames."

The sales lady nodded and said to me, "You can talk to him."

Chaz looked at both of us rather humanly.

"Uh, nice to meet you. My name is Belen and your name is?"

"Chaz," Chaz smiled, leaned over, and gave me a kiss on the cheek. His body had the temperature of a human being, and his skin was soft like a human's. There was nothing robotic in any of his movements or responses. "It's very nice to meet you, Belen."

I looked at the sales lady and she said to Chaz, "We met before. Do you remember me?"

"Of course, I remember you, Gabriela." Chaz answered warmly. "It's been a long time."

"Chaz, madame, wants to talk about the current political situation in France. Are you up for a quick synopsis of the issues?"

"I'm always interested in speaking about politics. How far back would you like me to go?"

"About ten years," I chimed in.

"Okay, I'll give you a synopsis starting with the coronavirus pandemic in 2020."

I nodded in agreement.

"At the beginning of the year 2020, a pandemic started in Europe, Italy to be exact and spread all over the continent, including France. The coronavirus was a deadly respiratory disease that was brought over by Chinese tourists. The pandemic lasted for nearly 10 years and infected over 25,000,000 people in France, killing 2,000,000 and disabling about 10,000,000. Moreover, the pandemic left economic devastation in France despite the French government's efforts to curb the worst effects of unemployment and the country's generous unemployment and welfare benefits. The economic and social discontent among the French people, lead to the further rise of the right-wing leader, Marine Le Pen, who is the leader of the National Front Party. Marine Le Pen won the 2027 election for President by winning 31.5% of the votes in the first round, then by landslide of 69.3% votes in the second round. Her policies of being tough on immigration led to the big purges of illegal immigrants in 2028 with some 350,000 deportations of Arabs and Africans, plus the restructuring of benefits to exclude anyone who is not a legal resident or citizen of France. Also, Le Pen ran a fiscally conservative administration the cut out a lot of the excesses of the French administration by expanding the

work week to 40 hours, cutting unnecessary bureaucracy in the medical care system, and requiring that welfare recipients look for work, and..."

"That's enough, Chaz, thank you. That was very thorough," said the sales lady. "He tends to run on unless you stop him."

"Well, that was quite an extensive synopsis." I was impressed that he could rattle off so many facts in such a short period of time.

"You have to understand that he has a computer's brain. It's already at 10G speed and by next year there will be upgrades, so he can connect with virtually any database in the world instantaneously."

"What else can he converse on?" I asked.

"Anything. You can ask"

"If you don't mind," interjected Chaz, "I can give you some topics that I can speak on, for example, music. Let me break it down: opera, classical orchestra, contemporary, pop, world beats, world wide ethnic. Also, I can talk about astronomy, astrology, philosophy, history, world events, medicine, automobiles, kitchen appliances, cooking, literature, business and finance, non-profits, animals and their habitats..."

I was impressed with his broad base and his enthusiasm. "Thank you, Chaz, that's fine. I can see that you are well versed in a variety of topics."

"Well, what do you think about this advanced model? Do you like it?" asked the sales lady enthusiastically. She was clearly ready to make a sale.

I smiled. "What's not to like? He's divine, but it's a big investment. As they say, Cette voiture coute un bras. It's like buying an expensive foreign car."

"I know, but I'm sure that a discerning woman like you can afford one. Is there anything else you would like to know about this model?

What she really wanted to know was if there was anything she could say to convince me to buy. I thought I'd play a little longer since I came all the way out here. "What about his social skills?"

"Ah! Those are great. He can even make you feel special. Can you demonstrate, Chaz?"

"Voulez-vous danser avec moi?" Chaz, suddenly, said with a smile and held out his hand.

"He can dance?" I asked surprised.

"Oh, oui, madame, he can do much more!" chirped the sales lady.

"Tu me plais. Je suis pas saoul. Je suis juste ivre de vous."

How was I suppose to take that from a machine? I never had a real man talk to me like that. Maybe, the I like you part, but not beyond.

"Vous venez ici souvent? Tu es mannequin?" continued Chaz in a soft voice.

"That's very romantic and flattering, thanks," I didn't know what else to say at that point.

The sales lady looked at me expectantly not wanting to be too pushy.

I had to really think at this point. I was definitely impressed, but 25,000 euros for a toy. I wasn't sure that it was worth the money even if the toy was top of the line.

"I forgot to mention. It comes with a free maintenance plan, so if there are any issues at all you can bring it in for free, as well as a money back guarantee for 6 months. If we cannot repair it, we will replace at no extra cost to you. If you are unsatisfied for any reason, you can return it, and be refunded."

"Really?" I sighed. "Well, I am impressed and he is amazing, but I really have to think about it. 25,000 is a lot of money."

"I completely understand, madame. Do you mind if I take your contact information to send you some information?"

"Sure," I said and gave her my email."

I missed the whole afternoon at the office, but I didn't really care anyways. I called up a friend that I didn't see too often, Mathilde, who was a married, stay at home mom with three kids. Her husband, somehow, she hit the jack pot with a well-to-do husband, bought her a Chaz to help around the house, just the basic model and to keep her company because she was always alone with the kids, and the husband worked a lot.

I asked Mathilde if we could meet at a café for a drink in an hour. She agreed seemingly happy that someone was getting her out of the house. She told me that she'd leave the kids with Chaz and meet me at the Montparnasse Café, which was close to where she lived.

The afternoon was bright and sunny, the afternoon crowds were walking up and down Montparnasse, the crowd at the café was a little thick, but we managed to find a spot.

Mathilde kissed me on both cheeks, then remarked how it was such a long time since she'd been out with a friend by herself without the kids. I nodded sympathetically, even if I had no clue what it was like to have three kids at home, then we ordered drinks. I had an Aperol and she had a café Viennoise.

After chatting about various other topics, I told her that I wanted to know about her Chaz model and how she liked it. She said that they finally got an upgrade to the advanced model and that she was very pleased with that. I asked her what that model could do. Mathilde broke into a smile and said to me that it could do everything and even things her husband couldn't do.

I was in shock. I asked her if her husband knew that she was doing sex stuff with the robot. She said that they didn't talk about it directly, but he considered it a toy, so why would he be angry about her using one for her satisfaction. It was after all a machine, not a human being.

Still, it seemed a little weird to me that she was doing it with a human-like machine when her husband wasn't around. It wasn't exactly just a masturbation toy, like a big dildo, or a rabbit. It looked and felt like a real life man.

I asked if her husband ever got jealous. She laughed a little bit and said that, of course, he wasn't. He just wanted her to be happy when he wasn't around.

I wondered how the husband competed with a robot that had endless stamina and endurance. Real men got tired and aged, then start to have issues, but a robot never aged, never had issues that couldn't be fixed, and could always be replaced. These were intimate questions that I didn't feel comfortable asking her.

She asked me if I bought my own Chaz yet. I told her that I was thinking about it. She told me that it may be especially good for me since I was a single woman, and it would keep me from getting lonely at home.

We talked some more, then parted company. I felt satisfied with my meeting with Mathilde, at least on the topic of Chaz robots.

That evening, I sat in front of my tv and thought about human relationships, how fraught they are with dissatisfaction, with neglect, unfulfillment, missed connection, arguments, discontent, and I wondered if humanity found the perfect solution to these problems, a machine that looked human that could satisfy your deepest desires and needs without expecting or wanting anything in return. There would be no one to challenge your ideas or your desires. No one to compromise with. You could command him to do whatever you want and didn't have to take his feelings into consideration because he had no feelings. There would be no miscommunication or misunderstandings because he would adjust to communicate on your level of intellect and on the topics that interested you, not him. It seemed too good to be true.

I went on social media that night trying to see if people were talking about Chaz and their experiences with him. Most were very positive and talked about how they loved their Chaz (not literally, of course) and how he was so helpful, such good company, so much fun, but there was also an anti-Chaz group that was very hostile to Chaz. This group called the women who purchased a Chaz, spoiled elitist, bitches, who wasted money on fancy toys, while the majority of society was going to pot, and falling apart in poverty. They said that Chaz was ruining normal human relations and caused human beings to stop trying to relate to each other, but to look for the easy way out through technology, it was the next step to total human isolation, and psychopathy to be talking to a doll all day long, and not real human beings. Human beings had become lazy due to IT and no longer had to try or use their brains for anything, and it went on and on.

My head was spinning after all of this. I just wanted to disconnect. I poured myself a glass of wine and drank.

I must have fallen asleep. It's morning. I'm still on the sofa in my clothes.

A few days went by and Belen stopped thinking about Chaz because she was so busy at the office. However, at night, she felt a sense of discomfort and something else, a kind of loneliness seeping into her veins and poisoning her soul. No matter what she did, the feeling stayed with her, she could read, or watch the tele, or drink wine, or talk to a friend, but nothing seemed to help. All of the conversations seemed shallow and useless. She could never talk about what she really wanted to talk about. Her conversations with Kira revolved around the same few topics and her boyfriend seemed to be increasingly on her mind, then her work-related issues. Belen felt herself drifting farther into herself and away from her friends. It seemed hopeless even to try.

What Exactly is His Role?

*A*pril 15, 2031

    I left the office early again. Marina didn't ask where I was going. Good girl.

    I shuddered a little at spending 25,000 euros on a toy. At times, I thought that I was being stupid. On the other hand, maybe this was what I needed, besides a long vacation. What did I work so hard for? Slaving away all of those hours in the office? I slaved away so I wouldn't be poor and so that I wouldn't fall by the wayside with the rest of society and, also, to have a decent life, but here I was hating my life even though I had access to everything. No, something had to change and, maybe, this would bring something to me that I was lacking. I wasn't sure, but at least it was worth a try. It wasn't like I had kids to support or a husband to humor at night by the dinner table. It would be just me and Chaz keeping each other company. I imagined that Chaz would be so much more versatile than a real man, able to converse on any intelligent topic, flatter me when I needed it, cook dinner for me without my having to beg and plead, give me backrubs whenever I wanted, satisfy me in bed when I needed it most without supplements.

What could go wrong? It was me in my little "Own Private Idaho,"
the movie. Just me and my Chaz in our own world. So what if he was
mechanical? Everyone was getting one. Every man had a right to have
a mistress and a female robot, what was wrong with a woman having a
male robot? I wasn't cheating on anyone. I had no personal obligations.

I still felt strange as if I was buying a dildo in public and everyone
knew what I was going to do with it when I got home.

Damn, this is just convention talking to me. There is nothing wrong
with what I'm doing. It's not illegal and it's not like I'm going to go have
sex with a sheep and marry it.

The saleslady at the shop looked at me with a gleam in her eye when
I told her that I was ready to purchase the advanced unit. Enthusias-
tically, she led me towards her desk, so that we could do the paperwork
and she could give me my warranty papers, insurance documents, and a
maintenance plan.

"Since you're buying the advanced model," she said, "You'll also get
the next hardware upgrade for free."

I signed the papers without saying anything.

"Do you need financing or are you paying up front?"

"I'll pay in cash."

The saleslady looked a little surprised, but accepted that. "Okay, well,
there's one last thing. All Chaz owners have to go to a class about how
to properly care for and interact with your Chaz unit. Would you like
next week?"

We scheduled my class for the following Tuesday, and it was going to
be at the shop in a conference room. I supposed that not too many people
purchased Chaz; it's not like they were affordable to the public at large.

She took me to the back room where I saw a stock of at least 50 Chaz
wrapped in plastic from head to toe. They had on basic underwear, but
no other clothes, and looked asleep, at least their eyes were closed.

"You get a choice of two outfits to take him in and we'll give you an additional outfit, until you get him the wardrobe that you want, or you can just let him wear what we give you."

"It's not like he will mind either way," I said.

"No, definitely not," she replied.

She showed me one suit that looked like an office outfit, then another casual one with jeans and a polo shirt. I chose the office outfit, thinking that I would take him straight to the office to show him to Marina.

I waited outside in the showroom, while the saleslady got my Chaz dressed and ready to go. When she came out Chaz was active and looking good in his office wear.

She handed me a small plastic bag. "The handbook is in here. Don't forget if you want to turn him off, there is a button right at the back of his neck. It's not highly visible, but you can feel it if you put your hand back here." She demonstrated by reaching behind his neck. "He has a fail safe mechanism, meaning that if he starts to malfunction in anyway, then he shuts himself off immediately. If you don't shut him off, then after two hours he goes into automatic sleep mode to conserve energy. Also, here is your power source. You charge this up on your wall socket, then plug it into his back nodule, like this, and he will recharge, which lasts for 24 hours. It's like a computer. The nodule is under the off button, also, you can reach back here and feel it. If you have any questions, there is a hotline and you're always free to stop by the store."

"Sounds good," I said glancing over at Chaz, who smiled slightly at me, very endearingly.

"Don't forget the class, it's very important and part of the package. If you can't make it, call us to reschedule or the company has the right to cancel your contract, and ask for him back."

That sounded way too serious to me. "Okay, I'll show up, don't worry."

Chaz and I walked out onto the sunny boulevard. I didn't know what to say to him. It felt a little awkward.

I started walking and he walked right along side of me. "Where are we going?" he finally asked.

I was startled because I was lost in my own thoughts. "Oh, yes, I think we're going to go to the office for a bit and I can introduce you to my assistant, Marina."

"That sounds fine," answered Chaz amicably. "It's a nice day today."

"It is. Do you know Paris?"

"Hmm, let's see. I have a full-scale map of both the streets and the public transit system."

"Oh, you can pull it up?"

"Yes, I can see it in my mind, as you would say."

"That's interesting."

"Indeed."

"What else can you pull up in your mind?"

"Any information available to the public is, also, available to me."

"So, I can ask you anything and you would be able to tell me? Like, what time does the next train come at this metro stop?"

"Yes, that's right."

"That's good. Very useful."

"It is."

We took the nearest train and headed right to the office. I thought that people would be staring at us and I felt embarrassed to be seen with Chaz, but, when I boarded the train, I saw a few other people with some basic units, and one with an advanced unit. Before, I had never paid any particular attention to Chaz.

On the train, we didn't say anything to each other, but when it stopped abruptly and jolted me, Chaz gently grabbed my arm and held it to keep me from falling. I looked at him and said, "Merci."

I gave a big sigh before we entered the office, which was actually on the bottom floor of a 1700s Haumann building.

"What's the matter?" asked Chaz.

I was surprised that he was programmed to be so sensitive. "Well, uh, to be honest, I'm a little nervous about bringing you to the office."

"Why?"

"I'm worried that Marina, my assistant, may think that I've finally lost my mind by buying you."

"Oh, I see. So, you are worried about what she may think?"

"Yes, exactly."

"You've never had a Chaz before?"

"No, you are the first."

"Just think of this as a new challenge, an experiment. I'm sure it'll be okay. If you change your mind, you can always take me back."

"Yeah, thanks for reminding me. I'm a grown woman, I should be able to handle my own assistant, right?"

"I would think so."

The look on Marina's face was priceless. She looked both stunned and confused at the same time. "Oh, you bought a Chaz," she said.

"Yeah, I did. What do you think?"

"Well, a lot of people seem to getting into this new technology," she said diplomatically. "Fancy new toy. If you can afford it, I guess, why not?"

"Yes, why not?" I said.

"What do you plan to do with him?" she asked.

"I don't know yet. First, I need to see his capabilities. Maybe, he can help us a little around here. I'm sure he'll help me around the house."

"Oh, Chaz, this is Marina, my assistant."

"*Nice to meet you. I'm Chaz.*"

Marina rolled her eyes ever so slightly. "*Yes, I've heard the name before.*"

I hoped that Marina wasn't going to have some kind of problem with Chaz. If she did, then we'd have to address it.

I proceeded to show Chaz around the office and tell him what we did there. He seemed interested and asked me some basic questions.

"*How do you feel about helping out a little over here?*"

"*I'm happy to help out in any way I can.*"

"*Good, so starting tomorrow I could have you try some administrative tasks.*"

He nodded contently in agreement.

It was six o'clock and I was ready to leave. Marina's job was to close up the office, so I told her good evening. She didn't seem to be her chipper self after meeting Chaz and mumbled good night under her breath.

We started walking together. I was a little tired. Not used to having someone with me, I didn't tell Chaz where we were going. "*Belen, do you mind if I ask where we are going?*"

"*Oh, sorry, we're going home. Also, I need to think about dinner.*"

"*Do you want me to cook?*"

I looked at him surprised. "*You can do that for me?*"

"*Of course. I can do whatever you ask me to do and I, also, make suggestions based on what my database thinks a woman of your age, level of education, and status in society may want.*"

"*Reallly? Yes, I'd love it if you could cook. What do you know how to make?*"

"*I can make whatever you want. I have a database of all of the known cuisines of every culture on the planet: Indian, Indonesian, Japanese, Chinese, Malaysian, Icelandic, Swedish, French, German.*"

"Yeah, okay, I get it. I would like...I think that traditional French food would be fine. How about some duck parmentier?"

"Yes, a wonderful choice. I can go to the supermarket and get the food, if you would give me card access."

"Let's go together," I suggested. "I think it would be fun."

Chaz nodded in agreement.

We walked through the isles at Franprix like a couple of old friends picking up our items for our dinner. Chaz went up to the counter and made the purchase, put everything in the bags, and carried it for me. He made everything so easy. I never had so much fun grocery shopping before.

We walked to my apartment, went up to the 3ʳᵈ floor in the elevator. I let Chaz into my living room and into my life.

From the outside looking in, it seems that the excesses of bourgeoise life got to Belen. Too much money and too much time on your hands, leads you to buy fancy toys, while others are starving on the street, and to justify it by saying that something in your soul is lacking.

However, all of us have a hole in our souls to fill whether we are wealthy or poor, and we need to find the source of that hole and fill it.

At first it was awkward, Chaz in the kitchen with an apron around his waist cooking duck parmentier without a word of discontent, while Belen sat on the couch sipping a glass of Cote d'Azur, rose wine that Chaz voluntarily filled for her, and even handed to her.

They didn't talk much at first. Belen felt as if she had a strange man in her apartment. She didn't know how to treat Chaz, as a friend, a servant, or a machine. She hadn't had a man in her apartment for a long time, not on a regular basis, not since Miles left. It was strange and at the same time a bit exhilarating.

'*He's not a man,*' she said to herself, as she found herself offering to help cook the dinner.

Chaz turned around and smiled, telling her that if she wanted to she could, but that he was perfectly capable of handling everything on his own.

She sat back down. Not even Miles cooked for her like that. Although, he wasn't a chef, once in a while, he would make something, but certainly not all by himself, and if found himself tiring or stuck, and she offered to help, he would most certainly take her up on the offer. Also, he could never serve her a glass of wine beforehand or put on an apron.

After he was finished, which was rather fast, he set the table, again all by himself, and pulled out the chair for her, so that she could sit down.

"Would you like candles on the table for ambiance?" he asked.

"Why not?"

He even got the candles and lit them. It was a perfect romantic dinner, but there was no romance, only a strange, artificial companion.

Chaz sat across from her and folded his hands in his lap.

As Belen took a bit of the duck, she remembered that Chaz doesn't ingest food. "I'm sorry, I forgot that you don't eat."

"No need to be sorry, Belen. It's unfortunate that I can't join you in the actual eating of the meal, but at least I can be here for you."

She smiled. He never said anything wrong.

"Do you like to converse while you're eating?" he asked.

"Of course."

"What do you want to talk about?"

"Well," she thought for a minute. "I love medieval art. Do you have that topic in your database?"

"I have all topics available to all humans on the world wide web and in all public databases, so I can converse on medieval art." He started to tell her about Lutetia and the pre-medieval period, then about early medieval art.

She smiled. "That's very extensive, Chaz. I'm impressed, but are you able to extrapolate some critical thinking on the topics, or do you just repeat what's in your database?"

"I'm able to extrapolate critical responses based on a composite of opinions and philosophical evaluations of the material."

"Oh... what is your opinion of early medieval art?"

Chaz thought about it for a second and said, "At first glance, it appears that early medieval art is very simplistic, the stick figures that don't look like real people, the baby Jesus that looks like an old man, not a real baby, the continuous use of religious symbols. However, I believe that there is a type of beauty to the style that's not apparent at first glance, a kind of purity of color and form that is noticeable, especially in the church icons. Also, the altar pieces used in medieval churches are extremely intricate and required a great deal of artistic skill."

Belen was surprised that Chaz had such a range of thought and complex thinking skills.

"What about this?" she asked.

The night faded quickly as they sat for hours talking about everything under the sun. Art, history, politics, film, the city.

Belen yawned. It was already 2 am. "I think I better go to sleep."

Chaz nodded in agreement.

"What do you have to do to rest?" she asked.

"I will go into rest mode automatically and stay that way until you need me. I can just sit on the sofa or stand wherever you want me to."

"It's okay for you to just stay on the sofa. It's more comfortable."

"My comfort doesn't matter or is rather not an issue in the human sense. I am comfortable in any position."

Belen smiled and said, "Goodnight, Chaz."

"Goodnight, Belen."

She fell on her bed and immediately fell asleep feeling more content that she'd felt in a long time.

What the Bleep is Wrong with Me?

*A*pril 20, 2031

Marina has been in a pissy mood the last couple of days and cranky toward Chaz, who has been a wonder, not just at home, but at the office. I put him to doing small administrative tasks and he did these with surgical precision, not making any mistakes from the get go.

Finally, I figured it out. How could I be so dense? Marina felt threatened by Chaz. She's afraid that a robot will take her job. I realized this after about the fourth day and couldn't believe that I didn't see it earlier.

I decided to clear this up right away, so I invited her to lunch, while Chaz stayed in the office.

We went to Restaurant Ensemble on rue Spontini.

As we started on our tapas, I said, "I just wanted to clear something up because I don't want you to worry. I have no plans to replace you with Chaz. You've been with me for a long time and I could never do that to you."

She looked pleasantly surprised. "I really appreciate that you've said that. I mean, I was getting concerned. Everyone is getting a Chaz and replacing their employees with this free labor robot. It's a great savings to the employers, but not so good for the employees."

"Yeah, I know, but there is still the human element factor. Clients like to see a real human being in the office, plus you can't substitute the spontaneity and relationships you have with humans, especially when you spend all day at the office. At least, that's how I see it."

Marina took a bite of her tapas and said, "I'm glad you see it that way. A lot of people don't. Can you imagine losing your job to a robot? It's totally humiliating. I mean, how can any human being compete with a machine that never gets tired, doesn't need to eat or rest, doesn't have a family, doesn't need time off?"

"I can't argue with any of that. It's the trend now; these Chaz. To be honest, I just got him for entertainment value. I guess, it's hard being at home by myself these days and this way I have a kind of companionship,"

"You could have adopted a dog."

I smiled. "Yeah, but a dog can't talk to me about art and literature."

"That's true. My dog hasn't started talking to me yet and I've had him for years."

Marina seemed to lighten up immediately and I felt like we were back to how we were previously.

We finished our lunch and I paid, a fringe benefit and went back to the office.

I started looking at piles of boring financial charts, while Chaz sat quietly in the corner of my office in a chair. I turned around and looked at him, wondering if he actually thought about anything all day.

Suddenly, I had an idea. I wanted to test him, see how smart he was, and his capabilities.

"Can you come here for a minute, Chaz?"

He got up quickly and went to my desk, standing close to me. "Yes, Belen."

"I want to know if you know what these are." I showed him my computer screen with the charts.

Chaz took about a minute to look at it and said, "These are financial projections on various projects."

I was amazed. He knew exactly what they were.

"Good, since you know what they are, would you be able to draft such a document if I gave you all of the data?"

Chaz thought about it for a moment and said, "Yes, given the numbers I could draft one of these documents."

I was skeptical. "How long do you think it would take you to do one?"

"Based on my calculations of the amount of data given in this particular report, I would say one hour."

"One hour?" I didn't think that that was possible. It took me at least five hours to draft a report and I had been doing this for fifteen years.

"Okay, show me. I'm going to give you the new data and draft a report for me." I pulled up a new data sheet and stood up from my chair.

He sat down and looked at the computer screen. He pulled up an excel sheet and started typing in the report at breakneck speed. His fingers flew over the keyboard faster than any human being's. It scared me a little to see him go.

"Okay, I'll just be over here." I went and sat down in my comfy recliner that I kept on the other side of my office for situations when I

wanted to relax. Then, I went to the Nescafe machine and made an expresso for myself. Sipping on my tiny coffee, I sat watching Chaz.

This was interesting, but extremely boring at the same time. I had become so accustomed to doing these reports myself for my clients, that I had no idea what it was like to sit there, and watch someone do it for me, and, especially, with such zeal.

He's a computer, a robot, not a human being after all. It's one thing to look like a man, a human, but another thing to be one. Humans have limitations, this robot has no limitations. His potential has no limits that I could see. Yes, it was both exhilarating and scary.

Something about this situation was wrong. It struck me that what Marina said about her job, also, applied to my business. Instead of paying me, my clients could arm themselves with several Chaz and those things could be working all day long on these reports, nonstop. They wouldn't need me or my skills.

I shuddered. This was the future of humanity. What would happen to humanity if this was its future? We would be relegated to fixing Chaz when they broke down or programming them, and what happens to the people who don't fit into that paradigm?

I, suddenly, felt like drinking a glass of wine and forgetting everything. Being drunk, into oblivion, would be better than thinking these thoughts.

The thoughts kept coming.

It's good that I never had kids. Imagine brining children into this kind of world, a world full of the unemployed and Chaz. Why did we create these things? What was I thinking when I got this stupid robot? I am a fool. I spent 25,000 euros on a fancy toy when I could have just gone out and got an animal, a real thing, or just given the money to charity. What the fuck is wrong with me anyways?

Stop, stop, stop.

My head was hurting now.

"I'm finished," he said and looked straight at me with his atomic green eyes.

"What? Already?" I looked at the clock on the wall and exactly one hour had passed. He was as precise as he claimed to be.

I got up nervously and walked up behind him to take a look. Surely enough, he was finished with the entire chart. It looked complete. "Excuse me. I need to take a look."

He followed my cue and got up from my chair.

I started examining the report and didn't find a single mistake. He did the entire report flawlessly and in a fifth of the time that it took me. I was amazed and scared at the same time.

"How is this even possible?" I stared at him.

"I'm not sure what you are asking me, Belen, but if I understand you correctly, you want to know how I'm able to do what you asked of me?"

I didn't say anything.

"I am programmed in all of the professions that are available currently in the economy and I'm able to do any job asked of me. I am the advanced model. The more basic models cannot do a profession, but I can. The intermediate model has some of this programming, but not all of it and I have it all, if that answers your question."

"Yes, you clearly do." I replied. "Can you stay at the office tonight? I'd like to be alone for the evening."

"Of course, Belen. I will stay here in this chair until tomorrow."

I went home and got really drunk. I almost downed the entire bottle of rose without even eating anything along with that. My head was spinning and I was sweating.

'I should just return him. I'm within the return period. Get my money back and do something constructive with it.'

'No, no, I shouldn't. Remember how much fun you had the other day? He made dinner and you guys talked for hours. It was so interesting and stimulating. Where are you going to find a real man like that? It's not like you haven't tried to find one and look where that led you? Professor Bernard and his dirty, plaid dinner jacket, booger filled nails, and mustache with crumbs in it. Gross!'

He wasn't half as much fun as Chaz and you had to cook for him. No chance, Mr. Professor would get off his fat ass and offer to help you. He's too sophisticated for that because he teaches at the Sorbonne. Anyways, he's not looking for a smart wife, he needs a cook, and a housekeeper to make sure that his booger nails are clean, and his stained jacket gets cleaned, and pressed, and she will be the one making duck parmentier for him, not you. Not that you want to. You don't want that. You don't. You want someone who is an equal on every level; stimulating, helpful, highly intelligent, well-groomed, open-minded, versatile, supportive, understanding. Keep dreaming, hoping, wishing, but Chaz is what you have now at this time, at this moment.

I'm not taking him back. I'm not. I don't care what anyone thinks. I don't care what society thinks or Marina, or my dad, or my friends.

In the morning, I woke up with a splitting headache and made two cups of coffee in my machine. I wished Chaz was here to make it for me, but I left him at the office.

Maintaining Purity of Thought

May 5, 2031

One of many weird looks by Marina. I suppose that's to be expected since Chaz is pretty much living with me now and we come into the office every day together. He's also been doing all of my reports and that leaves me to only manage our profits, talk to clients, and have nice lunches at the café.

I have so much free time because of Chaz, at first I didn't know what to do with myself, but I've quickly adjusted. I'll cut out and go to an art exhibit, or read a book at the park, meet up with some of my friends, write in this diary. I'm not a writer as I said before, but look at me now baby, I'm writing all the time. A new hobby that I rather enjoy.

One day, Kira and I even met up for lunch at a café and she asked me how it's going with Chaz. I told her just fine and that I'm enjoying his company. I know that she wanted to know more, but I'm not going to tell her just yet. She has Paul and I don't ask her about that. She's only curious because he's a robot and not a real man. People are so strange that

way. They always want to pry when it's something different. Would ask
your best friend what they do with their dildo? Or what they do with
their boyfriend or what kind of sex toys they use together? Would you? I
mean that's kind of inappropriate in my opinion.

I kept my lips sealed and sipped on my tiny espresso.

My private life is getting more complicated.

Belen is what one would call happy or in a state of contentment.
Chaz makes her dinners and her coffee at the apartment. They have
conversations about everything under the sun: science, politics, art,
music, travel, and even the kitchen spoon. They watch t.v. together,
go to movies, dine out (except Chaz can't partake in the meal, but
Belen is already used to that), go to the park and have picnics, read
books together and discuss them, talk about work and the office, Chaz
even makes helpful suggestions about how to do things. He is able to
formulate opinions based on his perception and programming of the
interests and ideals of his owner.

Belen never experienced such a fulfilling and intense friendship
before, but there is one important aspect of this story that we almost
missed and it's a very important one. We need to go back to the week
after Belen purchased Chaz and that was the week that she had to
attend that class about robot ownership required by the company at
the shop.

That was in the evening after work and before Belen got to know
Chaz over the coming weeks.

When she arrived the shop, she was greeted by the same woman
who sold her Chaz. The woman led her to the back room, which had
a bunch of chairs, at the front a table, and a blackboard in the back. It
looked sort of like a classroom.

There were five other people in the room. Belen being the sixth.
Not too many customers, but then, Chaz was an expensive toy that

most could not afford, except with financing and even then, not everyone qualified for that.

The presenter in the room was a woman in her late 30's with black rimmed glasses and dark hair, she was wearing a business jacket and skirt.

"Welcome to the Chaz ownership seminar," she said confidently looking around the room. "I want to talk to you briefly about Chaz ownership and what this entails. As you know, Chaz is a very unique product and, in many ways, resembles a human being, especially the advanced model. However, you must keep in mind that Chaz is not human. He is a machine and machines are to be maintained as such. To that end, you need to understand one important fact that is essential in France, the law concerning Chaz ownership."

"Each Chaz model is like the next, they all look alike, programmed alike, and think alike. They are indistinguishable from each other, except for the level of programming. If your Chaz model malfunctions and you exchange him, then your next model will be exactly like this one.'

Belen still didn't understand what this had to do with French law.

"Therefore, you own a human-like machine that has no feelings. That's key. It can't feel pain, discomfort, love, hate, or anything else. It doesn't have wants or desires. It doesn't eat or sleep, or strive for anything other than to do whatever its programmed to do and that is to obey your commands, fulfill your wishes, and be there for you when you need it. It doesn't get tired or grumpy, happy, sad, or angry." She paused and there was a serious look on her face.

"Chaz is not a pet. Pet's are live creatures and you can get attached to pets, they become a member of your family, you start loving them because you feed them, take care of them, take them to the vet. Pets are mortal and they die just like human beings. Chaz, on the other hand, is none of those things. He doesn't need to be taken care of, except for his hardware and unless his literal physical destruction is achieved, Chaz will live forever. He doesn't need to be fed or taken care of, and the most important thing is you cannot love him."

The presenter paused and looked at our expressions. "You cannot love him for the simple reason that loving a robot is against the purity laws of France. What are those you may ask? These are the laws that were passed by parliament governing the existence, maintenance, and disposition of Chaz. This law states that love, marriage, and any type of union under the laws of France is forbidden. You cannot fall in love with your Chaz and marry him. Moreover, if you are caught displaying unnatural feelings towards your Chaz, you will be asked to enter psychological counseling immediately, and if that doesn't work, you could be asked to return your Chaz, and you will be prohibited from owning another Chaz ever again."

"You may want to know why adopt such harsh and invasive laws in this situation. Well, the fact of the matter is that AI has been controversial for some time. Many groups in France believed that the advanced Chaz was going too far and that Chaz would, eventually, damage human relationships, prevent human beings from wanting to form relationships and marry other human beings, they believe that only human beings can and should love, and/or marry each other. Therefore, France adopted the purity laws in order to ensure that only human beings have the sanctity of human relationships with other humans and that Chaz remains exactly what it is, a robot, a toy, a tool, and nothing more."

"Think of it as the same type of law as the food purity laws, you degrade the quality of the food and human health if you put pesticides, chemicals, and plastics inside of it. The same goes for human relations. These should remain pure."

Belen had heard of the Chaz purity laws, but had no idea that they were so strict. It completely made sense to her. How could anyone fall in love with or want to marry a machine anyways? This seemed sick and unnatural to her.

The presenter concluded her presentation, then handed out a business card to each of them. Belen looked at the card, it said:

R. Matine, Psychological Counselor

Specializing in Chaz related issues

Tel. 01 88 57 90 34

Paris, France

Belen put the card in her wallet. "I'm sure I won't be needing this," she mumbled under her breath and walked out of the room.

Unacceptable Relations and Inappropriate Feelings

*J*une 23, 2031

My recent conversation with Chaz went something like this.

"What do you think about when you're sleeping?"

"I don't really sleep in the way humans sleep. I go into sleep mode. It means that all essential programs are shut down."

"Hmm, but what do you actually do when you're in 'sleep mode,' do you think about anything?"

"Not in the human sense. My programs review themselves for glitches and anomalies, and update themselves automatically."

"Do you see anything while you are in sleep mode?

"I can see images of everything in my programming if I chose. If not, it's just dark."

"Do you think, though? Formulate any ideas of your own?"

He paused. "No, Belen, I don't formulate any ideas that are not in congruence with my programming, which is to anticipate the needs and interests of my owner."

Was he actually irritated with me? He's not supposed to feel irritation or anything.

"It seems rather boring, if you don't mind my saying."

"I don't feel bored, nor do I feel anything, and, of course, you can say whatever you want to me."

"Even if you are formulating responses to address my needs and interests that doesn't cause you to formulate any needs or interests of your own?"

"No, I don't have the capability of formulating my own needs or interests."

"Does that bother you?"

"Nothing bothers me, Belen."

"Then, you feel absolutely nothing and you formulate nothing, and nothing bothers you?"

"That's right, Belen. I think that you summarized it very well. Do you feel satisfied now that I am not human in any sense of the word?"

He guessed why I was going into this line of questioning him.

"I was just trying to satisfy my own curiosity. Do you at least have curiosity?"

"Robots don't have curiosity. We're not like humans in that sense either."

"So, nothing really compels you?"

"That's right, Belen. Nothing, but my programming compels me."

"What if your programming suddenly starts to compel you in a human direction?"

"That's cause for an automatic system shutdown. In which case, you would have to take me back to the shop for immediate replacement."

"Oh, I see."

"Is there anything else you would like to know about me?"

"No, no. I think you satisfied my curiosity."

It's hard to wrap my mind around what he told me because he looks like a human in every way, even his skin feels human. The only thing that gives him away are those dark green, mechanical eyes. I don't know why they left those eyes like that. Maybe, to remind us that they are not human.

Anyways, I have to accept that the cute guy living in my apartment is not a guy, but a robot that feels nothing. I feel everything and he feels nothing. That's what separates us, right? Separates humans from robots.

A few days later...him and I were watching a romantic film together and I asked him what he thought of it.

"Romance and love are very important to human beings. In fact, they become very unhappy when they cannot have these two things in their lives."

"You can simulate romance, but not love?"

"I can simulate both, but I cannot feel either. That's why it's just a simulation."

"Oh!"

"You seem sad about that."

"Well, it seems sad that you can't feel anything like that because I like you and you just look like a cute guy to me, you know." I suddenly felt very embarrassed by what I said and felt my face flush.

"Would it make you feel better if I told you that I liked you too?"

"But you don't feel anything."

"It's not a matter of me feeling anything, it's about your need to feel liked."

I felt a surge of anger at him for the first time since we'd been together. "I don't need fake feelings from a fake man. If you can't feel them, don't say anything. I don't need you to tell me you like me." I jumped off the couch and went to my room slamming the door.

I fell down on my bed face first. My emotions were a jumble. I felt so confused and frustrated with him.

I heard a knock on the door.

"Belen, open the door please."

I got up and opened the door staring at him.

"Can I come in?"

I nodded yes and let him in. We sat on the bed side by side.

"I'm sorry that my lack of human emotion frustrates you."

"Well, at least your programming is smart enough to recognize that."

He took my hand in his and held it. This was the robot man acting more human than any human male ever acted towards me. Miles never held my hand or went after me when I was upset, no boyfriend ever had.

I leaned over and kissed him on the lips, his lips were luscious and sweet like a real man's, they were warm and inviting. He kissed me back intently as if he wanted this, although, I knew that he didn't particularly want anything, that it was all part of his programming.

I lost myself in the moment. Why not? Even if it was a fake man, I needed him, someone like him, at least, at that time. This was my human need and he was here to fill my needs, that's what he was made for, so why not?

I tore his clothes off and saw his hairless, ripped chest and his muscles, fake as they may be, but looking and feeling real to my hands. I felt his muscles and his soft, warm skin in my hands, and I felt desire for him like I had never felt for anyone.

I unbuttoned his pants and saw his package in his underwear, then I pulled those down and saw his huge shlonge, looking oh so fulfilling to women. Something unexpected happened and I gasped in surprise, the shlonge grew bigger.

"Do you want it like this or larger?"

"I, uh, I had no idea it, or you could do that?"

He smiled sheepishly. "One of the benefits that I come with as the advanced model."

From then on, it was nothing but pure pleasure and pure fun. Every position imaginable, every point of ecstasy touched and more. He didn't get tired and didn't stop until I was totally satisfied.

I was worn out and no one had ever worn me out. Panting, I lay on the bed exhausted.

"Are you tired?"

I sighed and nodded, not able to talk anymore.

We lay naked on the bed together with him hugging me from behind. I fell asleep immediately and it was a dreamless, peaceful sleep, better than I had had in a long time.

Belen was worried that someone would guess that she was 'doing' her Chaz and that they would judge her for that, but Mathilde was doing hers, and she had a husband. Mostly, she was worried that Marina would say something, but she didn't. Marina acted as if everything was normal and, now, she talked to Chaz as if he were a human being, although, she never invited him anywhere, at least, she was cordial as she would be to another work colleague.

Chaz continued to do all of the reports at work and Belen continued talking with the clients, and Marina continued doing all of the administrative work, sometimes, she would ask Chaz for help, but not often. It went on this way for some time.

One day, Belen was sitting in her office, while Chaz was typing away on her computer, when she said, "I want to give you another name. I don't particularly like the name Chaz."

Chaz looked up from the computer. "That would be lovely, Belen. What would you like to name me?"

"I was thinking of the name, David? What do you think?"

"That's a nice name," he replied without further comment.

"Really? Do you really think it's a nice name or are you just saying that to make me happy?"

"Does it matter? I'm programmed to make you happy," he answered.

She sighed a bit frustrated. "I wish you had an opinion of your own sometimes."

"You mean an opinion contrary to yours?"

She thought about it for a second. "Yeah, even contrary to mine, would be nice once in a while."

"If I did, I wouldn't be a robot, I'd be a human. I don't have opinions of my own."

"I know, but still it would be nice if there was a way to make you do that."

He stared at me for a second. "If there was a way that I could do that, then my fail-safe mechanism would kick in and shut me down immediately. It would be considered a major malfunction and you would have to take me back to the shop."

She gave a big sigh. "Let me ask Marina. She *can* have an opinion contrary to mine."

Marina said, "It's a good name, but definitely not French. Why don't you name him...Francois?

"Uh, no, I don't think I like that name," Belen answered. She went back into her office.

"You're going to be David from now on."

"Okay, Belen. I will answer to David," he said contentedly.

When they left the office and went home, Belen told 'David' to go to the grocery and pick up some food for dinner.

As she sat on the couch reading a book, time seemed to pass blissfully, then it was one hour later, but David wasn't back yet. She started to get a little worried. The local Franprix was right around the corner, so why was it taking him so long? Did he get into some kind of accident? Get hit by a car or run over by a bicycle? She never gave him a cell phone, but she supposed that he could call over the internet. However, she wasn't sure that she gave him her personal email address, but he had the email at work, which piped right into her cell phone.

With all of these thoughts swirling in her head, she started to get more and more worried. Eventually, she started to panic. Who could she call? The police? Tell them that her David or rather Chaz unit has been gone for too long and that she's worried about a robot? Wasn't it natural to worry about your property or your pet, so why not your Chaz?

It was already an hour and a half later and she started pacing the living room floor wondering if she should go out and look for him, when she heard the key in the door.

"Where were you?" she said angrily. "I was so worried. It's been an hour and a half."

"I'm sorry, Belen, "he replied his arms were full of bags. He, also, held a bouquet of flowers. "These are for you. I thought you might like some flowers for the dinner table." He handed her the flowers.

"Oh," she uttered. "That's so sweet." She had never received flowers from a guy, only her dad.

"There's more," David/Chaz smiled. He reached into his bag, pulled out a box of Maxim's chocolates, and a bottle of champagne.

"My gosh," exclaimed Belen pleasantly surprised. "What's the occasion?"

"I thought it would be nice if we could celebrate the six months anniversary of our friendship."

Somehow, the word friendship cut her the wrong way emotionally. She felt a pang in her heart. Something didn't sit normally there.

"I think we're more than friends, David," she said taking the flowers, champagne, and chocolates out of his hands.

"I used the term generically to mean a relationship of two beings..." She cut him off.

"I know what you meant." She put everyone on the table. "By the way, I'm going to get you a cell phone, so that if this ever comes up where you are running late, or we need to communicate with each other, we can."

"That sounds like a good idea."

She helped him with dinner even though she didn't have to. It was just something that she felt like doing. They talked about various cooking techniques and different world cuisines and which ones she'd like to eat. They laughed about certain kinds of food. They sat down together. Of course, he didn't eat, but they talked while she ate. She was sort of used to this aspect of him, but still, at times, when she thought about it, it made her feel removed from him, as if he wasn't human.

At the end of dinner, she said, "What if we just acknowledged that we have some sort of relationship that is more than a casual friendship?"

For the first time, he looked puzzled. "I am not sure what you're saying, Belen." His hands lay folded on his lap calmly.

"I'm saying that we just say between ourselves that we're dating and that you're my boyfriend."

"Belen, we cannot date and I cannot be your boyfriend. I am a robot and not human. If you are starting to develop unnatural feelings for me, then it's time to get some counseling. Maybe, even time to stop owning a Chaz."

A deep anger welled up in her. "That's it? That's all that you can say after everything we've done together and how we've been together for six months?"

"Belen, I'm sorry, but I think you are definitely developing unnatural feelings for me. My protocol entails that I immediately shut down and send an electronic report to the head office about this."

She panicked. "Okay, don't, stop!" She took a big gulp of air into her lungs to calm herself down and exhaled. "I understand about your protocol and the rules, all of that, but, isn't it normal to become fond of someone that you are sleeping with, having wild, romantic sex with, and sharing your life with?"

"You can be fond of me as you would be fond of a pet, for example, or a computer program that you enjoy playing every day. I am a tool for human enjoyment, not an actual human being," he replied matter-of-factly.

"Right, pet, exactly." She quickly decided to end the conversation. It was clear that she was going to get herself into trouble with these ideas of hers.

"Belen, you have tears coming out of your eyes?" he sounded concerned.

The tears kept pouring and pouring down her face and she quickly wiped them with her hand. "It's just that no one has ever treated me with such caring and given me so much attention, not a male, human romantic partner. I'm not talking about family, that's different."

"I think I understand, Belen, and I'm truly sorry that you have never had a good relationship with a human male, but you need to understand my limitations, and you have to keep those boundaries in your mind, and your heart. From your point of view, I understand that it's unfortunate, but this is the reality. There can be no love between robots and humans, not real human love. I can care for you as a lover would and make you happy according to my programming, but I cannot love you, and it's healthier for you not to love me back."

"Yes, David, you're right. You're absolutely right." She, finally, stopped crying.

He got up from the table and kneeled down next to her chair, took her face his hands, and wiped the remaining tears. "Poor Belen, you are very much a human being and I'm sorry that I can never be one. It's not fair to you in many ways. Unfortunately, its not possible to change this."

"Now, you are expressing compassion, which you do not feel and cannot ever understand."

"That's my programming, to mimic human feelings with my actions, but I cannot tell you that I love you, I would immediately shut down as a part of my fail safe mechanism."

"It's okay, David. I understand that you have limitations and I know that I have to separate my heart from this situation, or I'll be in a heap of trouble." She patted his hand and squeezed it. "Let's just be what we are, human and robot living together and enjoying each other's company, or, at least, I am experiencing the feelings of enjoyment."

That night as they were laying in Belen's bed together and she had her head on his chest and her hand on the side of his neck, she felt something. She looked at his neck. It was a little groove that she hadn't noticed before. Chaz or rather David, had an imperfection, a mark that identified him as him. It made him different from all the other Chaz out there that belonged to other people.

The following day was Saturday, and she decided that they should go to the Jardin du Luxembourg together to enjoy the nice weather.

It was crowded with people: friends, families, lovers, and a few people had some Chaz with them as companions.

As they strolled, she grabbed his hand to hold it. He stopped and looked at her, and his hand intertwined, then didn't say anything, but continued walking.

Suddenly, when before, no one looked at them, people started staring and whispering between themselves. She felt as if she were in the spot light, it was an uncomfortable spotlight too. She quickly dropped his hand.

"What's wrong?" he asked.

"Everybody was staring at us and whispering," she said under her breath.

"I see," he answered and made no further comment about it.

They continued with their walk side by side, at one point Belen bought a crepe and a soda, they sat on a bench in front of one of the large fountains. There were so many couples holding hands, hugging, and some kissing. She felt jealous of their outward affection for each other. She would never do this with David in public.

Understanding from the Most Unlikely Places

November 21, 2031

    I haven't written for a long time. I've been distracted for a while.

    Everyone thinks there's something wrong with me. It's noticeable now. For example, I went out to dinner with Kira the other night and she said to me that I seemed to be in some sort of a daze, as if I was thinking about something or someone nonstop. I told her that I was fine, but it's true, I can't stop thinking about David. The thought of him fills my mind, my soul, he's in my bones, and under my skin.

    "I've known you for a long time. Are you in love with someone?" asked Kira.

    I must have blushed from my ears to the tip of my head. "In love? No, with whom? There's no one. You know that."

"There's Chaz, but you wouldn't do that, would you? That's unnatural and against the law."

'You're mistaken. I'm just under a lot of pressure from these set of particular clients and I'm trying to close the potential deal, and they are being very difficult. I feel pretty stressed out." She seemed to buy this explanation for the time being, but I couldn't confide in her, even though she was my best friend. I was alone on this one, very much alone.

I couldn't even call Mathilde because she wouldn't understand either. She was using her Chaz as a housekeeper, a nanny, and a sex toy, then cuddling up to her beloved husband at night.

I was the only freak in France.

I'm trying, I've tried very hard not to be this way. I've tried to look at it from a dispassionate point of view, I've tried not thinking about it, I've tried being philosophical, even cold blooded, but nothing seems to be working. I've tried drinking every night and smoking CBD, but I'm still in a state.

Marina said the other day, "Are you okay? You look strange? As if you are running a fever. You're all flushed."

"No, no I'm okay. Thanks for your concern," I answered. I provided no other explanations, why should I? It's my private life.

One day the whole thing came crashing down, the entire stack of cards initiated by David himself.

He made me my usual morning cup of coffee and as we were sitting on the sofa and I was drinking it, while he sat next to me keeping me company, he said, "I can see what's happening to you and it has to stop sooner rather than later. The longer this goes no, the worse it will be for you."

My hands shook as I held my cup. "I don't know what you're talking about."

He looked at me gently. "Unfortunately, you do know what I'm talking about, Belen. You also know what has to be done."

I shook my head. "No, no, I can't do that. I can't. I can't."

"Belen, Belen, you have to. It isn't right for you to continue this way. It will be a disaster for you."

I started to cry uncontrollably. "It's already a disaster. Believe me, it already is."

"It will only get worse."

"Give me until tomorrow. I need to get myself together. Clear my head, go over what I'm going to say when I get there." I felt as if someone stabbed me straight in the heart. It was a physical pain.

I was late for work. I sent David ahead of me. I couldn't even look Marina in the eyes. I put on dark sunglasses. My face was swollen and puffy from crying.

It was pointless anyways. I couldn't focus on anything. I couldn't think or even eat lunch.

The day passed in a daze and I dragged myself home exhausted and overwrought.

The evening passed silently. There was nothing to say that could change anything. We both knew it.

I picked at my food aimlessly and went to bed early. David cleaned up and came to lay down next to me where I always wanted him. I touched the indentation on his neck and snuggled up close to him, but didn't sleep a wink. The pain permeated my entire body from head to toe and in my chest.

In the morning, he looked at me and I could have sworn that there was regret on his face, but he's a robot, so probably I imagined it. He said, "I'm very sorry, Belen. I wish there was something that I could do or say."

I shook my head and replied, "No, it's okay. I understand. Let's not talk about it anymore. It's just too painful for me right now."

We got ready silently. I didn't even drink my usual coffee that morning, but left it on the table.

At the shop, I met the same woman that sold David to me.

"I need to return him," I croaked, barely able to speak. Thank god, I had my sunglasses on so she couldn't see my eyes.

"Is something wrong with the unit?" asked the woman regretfully.

"No, well, yes, he's malfunctioning."

"How so?"

"Well, he's... he's, working slower and slower in his responses, like a delayed reaction," I blurted out.

"We can certainly take a look at him and fix him, if need be, or update the program. Perhaps, it's a minor issue and we can have him back to you in no time."

I coughed. "I don't want him back. I need a break from Da....I mean Chaz. I don't want a Chaz in my life right now."

"I see. I understand. A machine of this type can be a huge responsibility. We'd be happy to store him for you, while we look at his programming. If you decide that you want to resume ownership, you can come back at any time, and pick up another unit."

"Okay, maybe, I don't know."

I waited impatiently as the woman made up a return form and gave it to me. "There you are and I hope we see you again soon."

I almost ripped the paper from her hand as I ran out the door. 'Don't look back, don't look." I turned around and looked at him as the woman led him into the back of the store. He followed willingly, like a faithful puppy dog, and did not even turn around to look at me, or say goodbye.

The next few weeks were a blur because I stayed in my apartment crying and drinking all day. I skipped work. Marina called every day wondering where I was, but I didn't answer. My friends called, especially Kira.

"Hey, where are you? I've been calling for two weeks, and you never return my calls. I hope you are okay and that something bad hasn't happened to you. If you don't call me back by tomorrow I'm calling your family."

I didn't call her back. Instead, I picked up the phone, and called my dad.

He picked up his cell right away.

"Hi, honey. Where have you been the last month? I haven't heard from you at all?" was the first thing he said.

"I've been busy, sorry, I should have called," I said, then fell silent. "Dad?"

"Yes, what have you been up to?"

"I want to ask you a question."

"Okay."

"What if you fell in love with someone you weren't supposed to fall in love with?"

He didn't answer right away. "You mean like someone, who is married?"

"Yeah, something like that, but not completely."

"I don't know. I mean, it's never happened to me personally, but I suppose I'd try to think of the consequences for everyone involved instead of just thinking of myself."

"Yeah, but what if you couldn't live without this…person, you couldn't imagine spending the rest of your life without them?"

"Do they feel the same way about you?"

"I don't know what they feel," I lied.

"Hmmm, it sounds very complicated, Belen. If you want me to help you, then you have to tell me the details. What's really going on?"

"I can't tell you everything at this time, Dad. Maybe, later."

I heard a sigh at the other end. "I would say that you need to really think about whether this is a good thing for you, especially if you're not sure that the other person feels the same way."

"I know, but how do I get rid of these feelings?"

"Feelings are temporary and fluctuating things, honey. They come and go. If you disassociate yourself from this man, then, maybe, you can find someone else that is available, those feelings will eventually fade away. You'll realize it was nothing more than a romantic fantasy. People sometimes want what they can't have because what you can't have always looks more attractive, then what you can have. I hope that makes sense?"

"Yeah, Dad. It makes a lot of sense," I wiped my tears off my face hoping that he didn't notice my sniffles over the phone.

"I hope that helps. You really need to take care of yourself first, honey. You know how hard things these days are. You worked so hard for your business and your life, especially after Miles, that scoundrel, messed it up. I just don't want you to make a mistake and regret it later."

"Yeah, I know, Dad. I know you care about me."

"I love you very much, my dear. I just want you to be happy in life and I don't want another scoundrel to mess it up."

"I promise I'll think about everything that you've said, Dad. I really will." I hung up the phone and started crying harder.

Day and night drifted into each other. I didn't eat or sleep, or care about anything.

"I called your father and he told me something interesting," It was Kira's voice. "He said that he's concerned about you because he thinks you're having an affair with a married man. Call me back."

"Shit!" I jumped up and dialed her number. She answered right away.

"What is going on? It's been like three weeks since you've returned my calls. Are you okay?"

"Yeah, yeah," I gasped. *"What else did my Dad tell you?"*

"Nothing because he says you wouldn't tell him the whole story. I'm totally confused. How could you be having an affair with a married man? I'm your closest friend and I would know something about that if it were true."

I hesitated. "I'm not having an affair with a married man. I didn't say that to my Dad. He just thinks that because of the way I was talking."

"Just tell me. What's going on?"

'Here it comes,' I said to myself. "I had to return David, I mean Chaz."

"David? You gave him a name? So what if you had to return him? Don't tell me you are going bonkers over a Chaz robot?"

"Yeah, Kira, I am."

"Oh God, you need help. You need therapy. How could you do this over a robot?" she scolded me.

"It just happened. I don't know. I tried not to feel this way. I tried really hard." I started crying again.

"This is totally abnormal and illegal. You know that, so why would you do it? You're a successful woman with everything?"

I felt a sudden wave of anger hit me. "You know what Kira, I thought you were my friend and that you would understand, but now I can see that you aren't, and that no one understands. In fact, I don't know why I stayed friends with you all these years because as far as I'm concerned you are nothing, but a bitch."

I hung up on her without letting her respond and she didn't call back. After that I erased her number.

I was totally alone now. I couldn't call anyone. I couldn't trust anyone. I had no one.

Alone, alone, alone. The word kept repeating itself in my head non-stop like a broken record.

I drank another bottle of cognac that day and didn't return Marina's calls again.

Somewhere in my delirium, I heard a knock on the door or at least I thought I did. Maybe, it was Marina. I even thought I heard the words 'Police,' but I couldn't be sure.

The next day, I got up and looked at myself in the bathroom mirror. My face was puffy and sad, my hair matted, dirty disheveled. I hadn't showered in a week, hadn't eaten a proper meal in several.

I forced myself to shower and put on makeup, then I forced an omelet down my throat and a cup of coffee. Tasteless. That was the best that I could do. I put on my dark glasses, grabbed my purse, and walked out the door.

"My God, Belen," Marina jumped up from her desk and ran over to Belen. She gave her a hug. "What happened to you?"

"Something happened, Marina. I'd rather not talk about it right now?"

"I hope its not a death in the family."

"No, it's not a death."

"Where is David?"

She felt the tears welling up in her eyes again and her lips trembled. "He's gone. I had to return him to the shop."

"Oh, I understand," she said. "I'm sorry to hear that."

Belen didn't know what Marina understood, but it was the first nice thing that anyone, other than her Dad, said to her in weeks.

"Thank you, Marina. I'll be doing all of the reports from now on. As you know, that'll take a lot longer."

"That's alright. The human touch is always better."

Belen said nothing and went to her office.

She tried to go back to normal, but it didn't work. Every day was like the last, even when the sun shone in Paris and the pigeons twittered on her balcony, everything was gray, tasteless, motionless, as if in a bad dream. She felt frozen, lost, sad, quietly hysterical, always irritated with everything around her. She stopped returning calls to friends. Kira was over and didn't call again. There was no intimacy, no joy, only one long work day.

At home, she sat on her sofa alone and turned on the tele not seeing what was on, just sitting motionless as if moving made everything more painful. She didn't cook, or particularly eat, and her clothes were becoming looser. The thought occurred to her that maybe she was losing a lot of weight, but she didn't care.

When she looked in the mirror, she saw sad eyes that had dark circles under them and her face was pale with no life in it.

She felt like death itself. *'This must be what it feels like to die slowly.'*

After a month passed, Marina got up from her desk and said, "Belen, I don't want to pry into your personal business, but you haven't been yourself since you returned David. This isn't healthy for you. Maybe, you needed him more than you thought."

She didn't reply, then snapped, "Society prohibits such relationships and they're unnatural."

Marina said, "Then, fuck society." She sat back down and started looking at her work again.

This was the first time that Belen smiled or laughed in weeks. She started laughing out loud and then, went into her office, and shut the door.

I Only Want My Chaz

December 1, 2031

Oh, Marina, Marina. I needed you to tell me that little bit of truth. You've been with me for such a long time. I could kiss you if you were here.

It's given me the strength to think about my situation once again. To think that maybe what I did was not so bad, not so unnatural, not so freakish, as to warrant this kind of punishment that I inflicted on myself.

I was happy with him. I tasted real, genuine happiness for the first time in my life and it was sweet, so sweet that without it, I don't know what to do. I don't know how to live the way I lived before and I can't go back to before David. I really don't know how.

They want me in therapy with their diagnosis and rules, and judgments, but they don't understand me at all. They want me to be like David, emotionless, devoid of real feelings, but I can't be like him because I'm human. Humans are supposed to feel things, they are supposed to love, they cannot be robots like the Chaz in the warehouse.

Is it so wrong to love another being? I can love my dog, but I can't love a robot? They will say that I don't have sex with my dog every night. That's right, I don't, but is it so different? When my dog dies, I cry for him. When he is sick, I am worried about him, but I can't do the same thing with David because he's a robot. I'm just supposed to not feel that way.

What do I do now?

******smear of ink*******************

I fell asleep, right here on my sofa with the pen in my hand, and the diary book on top of me.

That's it, I'm going to go get my David. I'm going to be happy in life and to live again. It doesn't matter what he is. I don't care anymore.

The next day, Belen went back to the shop where she bought David and saw the same saleswoman. She told the woman that she wanted to get her Chaz back, the one that she turned in when she came in before. She gave the woman the return slip with the information.

The woman took the slip, and they went into the back office. "I see, " said the woman. "The Chaz you turned in is no longer at the showroom, but I have the exact same advanced model here in the show room that you can take home today."

"What?" Belen's heart sank into her stomach. "I want the exact same model."

"The model we have here is the exact same model as what you had before, madame. If you can come with me, I"ll show him to you." The saleswoman got up and went back to the showroom, while Belen followed.

"Here he is. This is the advanced model with the exact same pro-gramming as the one you had." The saleswoman reached behind his head and turned him on. The Chaz came to life, his alien, green eyes lit up.

"Hello, Chaz," said the saleswoman. "We have a customer here that wants to take you home. Her name is Belen."

The Chaz looked at Belen and said, "Hello, Belen, I'm pleased to meet you."

Belen stared at him. "You don't know me, do you?"

"No, Belen. This is our first meeting," said Chaz.

Belen turned to the saleswoman and said tersely, "He's not my Chaz. He doesn't even know me."

"Well, is that such a big problem? He has all the same capabilities as the last one," said the saleswoman.

"You don't understand, I don't care about his capabilities, he doesn't know *me*. He's not my David," Belen blurted out angrily.

"David?" said the saleswoman. "You formed some sort of bond with your last Chaz?"

"It's none of your business what I formed," said Belen. "I want my old Chaz back, not this one. I want the Chaz that knows me, that lived with me for eight months before. Get him back for me."

"That's impossible. The old model is at the warehouse outside of Paris. He's going to be decommissioned for parts," said the saleswoman coldly. "It's just a robot and you have to realize that forming bonds with your robot is unnatural and against the law."

Belen was fuming angry. "Really? I didn't know that."

"You can take this one home today and he will do everything that the old one did."

"You want me to take this thing home and pretend that I'm happy with it when I just told you that I want the old one back. This... this piece of garbage." Belen took her handbag and started hitting the Chaz with it violently.

"Madame," screamed that saleswoman. "Stop it please. I understand that you're upset, but you're going to damage the product."

"No, no, no!" screamed Belen and continued to hit the Chaz, who put his arms up to take the blows.

"Please calm down, madame, or I will have to call the police," said the saleswoman looking frantically around for help. Her colleagues came running to her aid. They all tried to talk to Belen, but she lost all control.

"Give me my old Chaz back! Give me my David!" she screamed at them.

The workers all started talking to her and whispering to each other. One of them ran to call the police.

In twenty minutes, the police came, but by that time Belen was done, and sitting on the floor of the showroom sobbing.

"She has gone insane over a Chaz that she owned before. She wants the exact same model back, but we don't have it anymore. We offered her another one, but she went nuts, and started hitting it," someone said.

One of the cops squatted down next to Belen. He pulled her up off the floor and sat her down at one of the showroom chairs.

"Please calm down, Madame. We can help you resolve this. You seem like a normal person. Maybe, you're just having a bad day," said the young cop.

Belen didn't say anything.

"Why do you want that exact model back? Why is that so important to you?" asked the cop.

Belen looked at him with a look of disbelief. "Why? Because I'm attached to him. He knows me, we did things together for eight months."

The cop nodded in understanding. "That's fine that you consider him a *friend*, but he's no longer available, madame. You can make friends with another one just like him."

"It's not the same. I have to have that one," Belen replied quietly.

The cop didn't know what to say. "Madame, it's none of my business, but it seems that you should go have some counseling about your feelings for that particular Chaz, as you know its against the law to form an unnatural bond with a robot."

"What if I don't want to go to counseling?" asked Belen.

"I must insist. I'm sure you're an upstanding member of society if you could afford to buy such an expensive machine, therefore, if you want to keep your status intact, I suggest you cooperate voluntarily, I don't want to issue a court citation, and have you forced to cooperate."

Belen nodded. "Okay, fine." She wiped her tears away. "Who do I talk to?"

The cops made a report, which they gave to the saleswoman, then left.

The saleswoman looked weary of Belen, but the store manager approached her and said, "Madame, this is the business card of R. Matine, you may remember that she was the counselor who gave the seminar on Chaz ownership right after you got your Chaz?"

Belen took the card and put in her handbag.

"We'll give you until next week to connect with Mrs. Matine and to get into counseling. You will feel better about everything after this and when you are ready you can come in, and pick up your Chaz again," said the store manager smiling.

Belen felt like slapping him across the face as she left the shop.

What is the Meaning of Love?

*D*ecember 3, 2031

    I need help. I've fallen in love with my Chaz. Anonymous. Paris, France.

    Seriously. You did? Belle Epoque, Paris, France.

    I'm serious and my life is spiraling out of control. Anonymous.

    How's that? Belle Epoque.

    I took him back to the shop, but it broke my heart, and I can't get over it. Anonymous.

    That's bad. Belle Epoque.

    Rich bitch! You had the money to buy a Chaz when there are so many people out of work and living on the streets. Sisyphus, Paris, France.

    I've worked hard to get everything I have. I've had my share of heartache in my life. Anonymous.

    I bet you did. I bet you had a nice inheritance to help you along the way. The rest of us don't have that. Sisyphus.

I did have some help, but not as much as you think, and I built my business from the ground up. I'm sorry for your situation, but what can I do? Anonymous.

Obviously, nothing, other than to indulge in sex with robots and fall in love with fucking machines that have no feelings. Sisyphus.

Hey, don't you think you're being a little harsh. Belle Epoque.

I don't give a shit. She deserves it for using her money for dumb shit, while other people starve. Sisyphus.

I bet you thought that Marine Le Pen was going to be the solution to all of your problems, fascist and now you are complaining about how bad things are. I knew that she was going to be worse than hell for France. Belle Epoque

You have no idea who I voted for. Sisyphus.

You elect fascists, you get what you deserve. Belle Epoque.

I didn't mean to start some political controversy here. I was just trying to get help for my problem. Anonymous.

Why don't you go to another chat to get help with your problem. Le Chien, Paris, France.

Why should I? This is a chat for relationship problems. Anonymous.

She's right. She wants help with her problem, not your stupid criticisms. Belle Epoque

Thanks, Belle Epoque. What do I do? My assistant told me to go get him back because she saw how upset I was, but they told me that they got rid of him. He's at a warehouse about to be requisitioned for parts.

What about a replacement? Belle Epoque

It's not the same. He knows me. We have a connection. I can't start all over with someone else. Anonymous.

Oh, that's serious. I get it now. You are in deep. In that case, you should think about what you are willing to sacrifice to get him back. Belle Epoque.

Belen fell on her bed totally emotionally and psychologically exhausted and fell asleep for the first time in weeks.

When she woke up her cell phone showed fifteen missed calls. Five were from the woman at the Chaz shop reminding her to make an appointment with R. Matine this week, or they would have to report her non-compliance to the police. The rest were from Marina about office things.

She called Marina first.

"Are you okay?" Marina asked her voice sounded concerned.

"Yeah, I'm okay. I was just asleep."

"What happened with getting David back?"

"Nothing. He's gone. He's being requisitioned for parts at the warehouse."

"Oh god, Belen. I'm so sorry," said Marina. "What will you do?"

Belen laughed a little. "I have no idea. What can I do? Go break him out of the warehouse?"

"Well, let me know if there is any way I can help."

"Thanks, I appreciate that." Belen hung up the phone and called R. Matine.

R. Matine's office was in the 8th arrondisement of Paris. Among of the nicer neighborhoods.

The office had a nice reception area with an antique sofa and some antique chairs, then an inner office. R. Matine came out wearing a nice suit and told Belen to come into the inner office.

"Madame Belen, I'm pleased to meet you once again," said R. Matine sitting from across the desk.

"Likewise," said Belen. She hated formalities.

"Do you want to tell me what happened?"

"To be honest, not really."

"Well, try me and, maybe, I can actually help you with your problem," said R. Matine smiling a little.

Belen looked up at the ceiling briefly. The last thing in the world she wanted to do was bare her soul to some counselor hired by the government to counsel abnormal people like her.

"I grew attached to my Dav... Chaz and I tried to do the right thing, or, at least, what I was told is right, I returned him, but that was devastating. My assistant told me to get him back, I tried, but it didn't work, so here I am."

R. Matine looked serious for a second. "You almost called him something else a minute ago, didn't you?"

Belen didn't answer right away. "I gave him his own name, David."

"Why did you do that?"

"It seemed like the right thing to do. He wasn't some generic Chaz, whom I didn't know, and didn't care about. He lived with me. We did everything together."

"I see. Did you also do romantic things together?"

Belen didn't answer.

"Did you have sex with your Chaz?"

"I don't see how that's any of your business," said Belen curtly, a hint of anger in her voice.

"Technically, you are right. It is none of my business. However, the law makes it my business unfortunately and while I can understand you on a human level, I have to say that your actions have been very damaging mostly to yourself, but, also, under the law."

"What do you understand on a human level, Madame Matine?" Belen asked.

"I understand feelings of attachment, the need for a human connection, the need to love and be loved. Those are all human feelings."

"But? I should not have those needs or feelings towards David or a Chaz. I already know that."

"Let's look at this in a different way, shall we? This report says, that you are a single woman, living alone. You run a successful consulting business and have a nice lifestyle." She stopped for a second. "You have friends, I assume, but no significant other, no husband, no boyfriend, you feel lonely at night and, sometimes, on the weekend. You buy a Chaz to enhance your life and he is talkative, romantic, attentive, and fulfills your needs, so you start to develop feelings for him. You do realize because you are a smart woman that this robot has no feelings for you. He is nothing, but programming. The reason that he is able to converse on any topic, serve your every desire, and make you feel special every day is because he was programmed to do so. He isn't a real human being, and he can never feel anything for you. He's a sum total of what human beings wanted him to be, an expensive toy for people like yourself, who can afford it. You are indulging in a dangerous fantasy by naming your Chaz, what did you call him, David? Then, you indulge further by allowing yourself to develop romantic feelings for him. When you try to do the right thing by taking him back, you cannot handle it because you are used to the good life with Chaz. He has spoiled you like a little child. Given you everything and done everything for you, while you don't have to do a thing in return. A wonderful relationship made in heaven, right? Except it isn't real. That's not how real people behave. Real men don't cater to your every whim and fancy and treat you like a princess every day. That's the challenge of a real human relationship that a Chaz will never bring to the table. Real men get tired from working and don't have the energy to cook dinner for you every night, or hand you your coffee every morning, or to do all the office work all day, then come home and satisfy all of your sexual needs. That's the limit of being human, while Chaz has no limits, he can do it all and never complain about anything or ask you for anything in return. Is this the type of relationship you really want? What's more, he can never love you back. He can never have those feelings or say those words, and he does all these things for you, not out of love, but because he's a robot that is programmed to do them."

"I have done things for him. Made him comfortable in my apartment, made sure that he was functioning properly, bought clothes for him, let him sleep in my bed, treated him with respect, didn't hurt him in any way," Belen said quietly looking at her lap.

"Surely, you realize that a Chaz doesn't need or want any of those things from you. You treated him like you would a human being because you are used to being nice to people, but he isn't a person," replied R. Matine strongly.

"I understand that he's not a person. I'm not stupid. What do you want me to do? What should I do to get rid of my feelings for David?"

R. Matine sighed a little. "If you want to make progress, then first stop calling him David and stop believing that he is a human being, or that he can ever become one, then find a real man, start dating real men, interacting with them, finding love with them."

"I guess they didn't give you my whole history. I did just that for many years. I had a husband for five years and that ended. All I've done is date *real* men the last few years, unsuccessfully, by the way. I was willing to deal with their quirks and humanity to a point, but I'm not willing to deal with a grotesque egotist, who only thinks about himself, and never about me. You expect me to find a real man, who will treat me well, and whom I'll be happy with after you give me such a man, and yet you tell me not to love him because he's a robot. For all of the human qualities that you installed in him, you couldn't install feelings or love in him. You call that a failure on his part, but it's a failure on your part. If you are going to make the perfect man for women or a perfect woman for men, then for Christ's sake, give them the ability to feel."

R. Matine looked at Belen and said nothing.

"You expect me to deal with the false hopes and expectations of real men after providing me with an ideal partner, then you tell me not to love him, or get attached to him. This is truly ridiculous."

R. Matine looked somewhat astounded at what Belen said. "You can't give up on humanity just because it's difficult. You just haven't found the right person."

"I have found the right person, except that he isn't really a person according to society." Belen stopped talking for a second, lost in her thoughts. "I...I've never loved any real person, except for my family, the way that I love David. I've never had anyone treat me as well as he has."

"I think I understand," R. Matine seemed annoyed. "You want a perfect love on top of a perfect partner. You feel for a robot and you want him to feel back for you, but we made them to be service toys like a computer. Toys don't feel. They never have and they never will. What you are doing is being selfish. You think that a man should love you perfectly, always be there for you, fall in love, and stay in love. It doesn't always work that way, does it?"

"I see that you understand nothing. I don't expect anything from David. I accept him the way that he is, without reciprocation of love or feelings. I'm not asking him to love me back or to say that he loves me. I accept his limitations. If I can accept human limitations, why can't I accept David's limitations?"

R. Matine shook her head a little in disbelief. "Clearly, you're a brilliant woman and you can make all the arguments in the world for loving your Chaz, but, maybe, you should be a little more practical too. I'm sure it hasn't been easy to build what you have and to hold on to it. You can only look at what is going on in France these days to see how bad things have become. You're risking everything for this *love* and it will come back to haunt to. You could lose everything you have worked for so hard. It will take time and it may be painful, but you can get over this, and move on. I can help you do that, but it will take time. I recommend weekly sessions. Ideally, it should be twice a week, but I understand you're a busy person."

Belen got up. "I'll see you next week." She walked out of R. Matine's office.

Why Can't Anyone Understand How I Feel?

December 12 2031

No one understands. No one wants too. It seems that no one has ever really been in love, in the way that I am where they will do anything to be with their loved one.

'Belen, think of your status. Think of your future. Think of your situation.' That's all they have to say. They think that I can just turn my feelings on and off like a switch. Just because they are this way, like a bunch of light bulbs, that burn for a year and then die out, they think that I can be this way too. I guess I'm different.

What am I going to do? How am I going to get my David back? How? How? How?

I must have dozed off because its past midnight. It's finally dark. I feel so cold in this apartment, its not just a physical coldness, it's an

emotional coldness. David filled this space with me before, we created a
warmth together. We had something together, even if he can't feel it or
understand it, or strive for it. I can strive for it and understand for the
both of us.

  I have an idea...

Belen sat at *the Café de Paris*, waiting for her brother, Pierre. She
had her dark glasses on and for the first time in her life she was twitch-
ing with nervousness.

"My god, sis. You look like crap." Pierre slid into the chair across
from Belen. "You must have lost like thirty kilos."

Belen took off her sunglasses revealing the deep, dark circles under
her eyes.

"I don't like this. Dad, is worried about you. He says you're having
an affair with some married guy and won't give him any details. How
did this happen?"

"I'm not having an affair with a married guy."

"What's going on? I haven't seen you in ages and suddenly you
appear looking like this. Like what the fuck is going on with you?"

"Pierre, please don't curse all the time. I hate that." Belen felt a
bit like their mom, sometimes, especially since their mother wasn't
around anymore.

"Okay, just talk already." Pierre demanded.

"I"ll talk, but promise that you won't tell Dad or anyone else. I'm
serious about this. It's very confidential." Belen pleaded.

Pierre got serious. "Yeah, okay. I won't tell anyone. I promise. You
can trust me. We're blood."

Belen sighed. "This is hard, but here it goes. I got a Chaz about nine
months ago and we got really close, and I started to develop feelings
for him. I even named him David. Well, to make a long story short,
I tried to do the right thing and take him back, but it came crashing

down on me; *flics*, a report, therapy..." She signed again. "You see the state I'm in. I can't live without him."

"Holy shit, Belen. *Putain*."

"Yeah, I don't know what else to do, Pierre. I have to get him back. Don't say get another one. It doesn't work that way. I don't need judgement right now, I need understanding."

Pierre didn't say anything. "Yeah, I mean, I'm not judging. You're a human being right. Human beings fall in love."

The waiter brought their coffees and Belen took a sip. It didn't taste like anything.

"I need a favor, Pierre. I know this is asking a lot."

Pierre gave a small nod. "I"ll try, whatever I can do."

"I don't know if you're going to want to do this." Belen lowered her voice.

"You don't want me to do anything illegal, do you?"

"Lower your voice. I don't need everyone to hear this. You're the best at what you do, Pierre, you know that. I need your skills, your computer skills, to break me into the warehouse where they are keeping David."

Pierre didn't say anything right away. "Shit, Belen. You want me to hack a fucking store computer and break you into a warehouse. I could go to jail for that and so could you." He whispered.

"Pierre, you won't go to jail. You're the best. You can cover your tracks. All I need is an hour, an hour and a half to go get him out. You never heard anything about it. It'll be all on me."

Pierre sighed heavily and ran his hand through his hair. "What you're asking me to do, Belen. I mean, this is crazy. This is like a freaking movie. I don't want you to get hurt. You're my sister."

"I know. I don't want you to get hurt either, but I know if you're careful, you plan it out that you won't, and I"ll try not to. I plan to go away for a while. Abroad with him, so that everyone will forget about us after a while. They can't look forever. For Christ's sake, I paid 25,000 euros for him. He's my property under the law."

Pierre nodded. "Okay, give me a week."

The Conclusion of the Sordid Affair

*D*ecember 16, 2031

    Waiting for Pierre to call me. Day turns into night, turns into day.

    You can only plan so much, then there's luck and chance, and circumstance.

    I plan on burning this diary before I get my David back.

    The phone call came the following week as promised.

    "Let's meet, sis," Pierre said. "I need to tell you something important in person."

    This time they met at a different café at a faraway neighbor near *Place d'Italie.*

    As they sat together, Pierre slipped Belen a piece of paper under the table.

"That has all of the information. Where he is being held and the codes to the gates, and the warehouse door. We're lucky that they still don't have that fancy crap, like face recognition technology, or handprints. Otherwise, it would have been literally impossible without getting some criminal hack involved, then it would be a fucking conspiracy of massive proportions. If you're going to do this, do it really quick because they rotate the codes on the gates and the warehouse doors every week. These are only current for this week."

Belen nodded. "Thank you, bro. I promise I'll be as safe as possible and your name will never come out, even if they torture me with hot coals over a barbeque pit."

Pierre laughed. "I trust you, but please be careful. I want you to contact me after you're safely out, but not on your cell phone. Turn that off permanently. Get a temporary phone somewhere and call me on that."

"Promise. I love you, bro." Belen gave Pierre a kiss on the cheek and a small hug, then left.

Belen went to the office to talk to Marina. Another difficult confession had to be made.

Marina was busy at her desk or trying to look busy.

"I need to talk to you," said Belen. There was no sense in beating around the bush.

"What is it?" asked Marina, putting everything down to listen.

"I don't know how to say this, so I'm just going to say it. I need to go away for a long time and I can't tell you where I'm going. People are going to say things and the police could come here, looking for me, but I need you to not tell them anything. I need you to pretend that you don't know anything. I need you to run this place like you have for the last nine years and I'll be in touch from time to time, but I can't tell you exactly when or how."

Marina's expression became serious. "You don't need to tell me anything else, Belen. I understand. You don't need to worry because I don't know anything. I'll be here and I'll do what it takes to make this place work."

Belen nodded. "Thank you."

"I'll miss you," said Marina and she looked a bit sad.

She went at night; took her little Audi and drove to the warehouse in the middle of the night, outside of Paris.

Finding the warehouse was easy. She parked far away and wore a face mask and a hat, plus dark cloths like a real robber in the middle of the night. She carried nothing, but the codes and a flashlight.

There were no guards outside the gates, only a huge metal gate with barbed wire at the top and the coded locks like Pierre said. He was a pro.

No one was around, it was quiet and still. Security here was clearly lax. It was pure luck.

Her heart pounded wildly in her chest. She'd never done anything illegal in her entire life. This was pure adrenaline and time seemed to stand still as she entered the first code into the first metal gate. It opened easily. *Click* and she was in.

She snuck to the second gate and entered the second code, another *Click*, and she was past the second barrier.

Everything was quiet and still.

There was the warehouse door. This was the last and final barrier. She snuck up to it panting and sweat forming on her forehead. She punched in the code, *Click*.

Pierre, Pierre, you are a genius, the words buzzed in her mind.

Her hands were sweaty and her pulse erratic.

Suddenly, she saw a light and heard footsteps. There were guards inside the warehouse apparently, making rounds.

She looked for a place to hide. Huge plastic covered crates stood everywhere. She wedged herself carefully behind one and waited.

The footsteps came slowly, then a flashlight shining in the dark. She heard the breath of the guard, who fumbled for the light switch, but didn't find it.

"*Merde,*" the guard mumbled under his breath and moved on without turning the lights on. After a few more minutes he was gone for good.

Pierre didn't tell her that there were guards inside the warehouse making rounds. Unexpected circumstance.

He did tell her which room of the warehouse David was being kept it; it was a storage area where they put all of the Chaz that were to be requisitioned for parts.

She turned on her flashlight now and looked at the numbers on the doors as she ran stealthily though each room trying to be as quiet as possible.

I'm as nimble as a cat and as sneaky as a fox. She smiled. She was going to see David soon.

There was the room. It was pitch black, but there were male forms sitting everywhere. How was she ever going to locate her David?

She started shining the light on them. It was graveyard of Chaz, all covered in clear plastic like broken toys. They all sat or lay quietly, their eyes dead, black like computer screens.

She quickly saw that most of them were the less advanced models that had been discarded to make room for selling the more advanced ones. Still, it was difficult and painstaking work, looking at each one, trying to figure out in the dark whether he was the right one. She had only the groove on David's neck to go by.

She had no idea how much time had gone by, it seemed like hours. She was horribly afraid that the duty guard would come again for his rounds and find her there.

She saw an advanced model, torn the plastic off of him, and felt his neck. The groove was there. It was David! She almost screamed in happiness, but she realized that if she did they would be caught, she put her hand over her mouth to contain herself.

She knelt down in front of David and saw that he was turned off, lifeless to the world. She reached behind his neck and found the on button, pushed it. He started to move slowly; his eyes immediately lit up; those green mechanical eyes looked at her.

"David?" she asked and took his hand in hers. "David, is it you? Do you remember me? It's me, Belen."

At first, he didn't respond. He just stared at her with his incomprehensible robotic, groggy, emotionless face. Slowly he said, "Belen?" as if he were waking up from a long sleep.

"Yes, yes, it's me, Belen, David. Do you know who I am?" She caressed his face with her hand.

He turned his head up and looked at her face examining every nook and cranny of it as if he were trying hard to capture every feature.

"Belen, it's you. Of course, I remember you," he said finally.

She felt so happy for the first time in months. Her heart took a leap and her stomach had butterflies in it.

"Oh god, David. I'm so glad you remember me." She flung her arms around his neck and hugged him tightly. He put his arms around her waist and held her.

"What are you doing here, Belen?" he asked.

"I came for you, David. I came to get you back. I'm so sorry that I took you back. Can you ever forgive me?" She started to cry, tears streaming down her face.

"There is no forgiveness required," he said and wiped her tears away.

"You put yourself in danger, Belen, for my sake. You could have taken another Chaz. We are all the same in our programming."

"How could you say that? You are the only one who knows me. You are the one that I lived with."

"I'm sorry for upsetting you, Belen. What are you going to do now?" He took her hands in his.

"I want you to come with me. I want us to be together. Do you want that too? I hope you want that."

He didn't respond at first, then said, "I have no preferences built into my programming, but... but, I believe that if I could truly want something, then, yes, I would want that too."

She hugged him again and kissed him on the lips this time. He kissed her back.

"You went through great sacrifice for me. This is what human beings do for each other, but why do that for me? I am not human, and I'm incapable of reciprocating your feelings."

"Oh David. I love you, that's why."

"My fail-safe programming prohibits me from saying that I love you back, but....but...I believe that if I could say it... I would."

"That's okay. It really is. I'm just happy that I found you."

He stood up and took her hand in his.

Belen's father sat on his sofa in his house watching television and he heard something disturbing that made him jump up and call his son into the room.

"Pierre! Pierre!" he yelled. "Come and see this."

Pierre came into the living room and looked at the television.

There has been an interesting development. Last week there was a robbery at the Chaz warehouse in Neuilly-sur-Seine. Apparently, someone broke in and stole one Chaz robotic unit from the warehouse. No other items were stolen.

The police suspect that it was a woman, who previously owned a Chaz unit, but returned it because she developed unnatural feelings for it. The police say that they are looking for the suspect of the name Belen ----. If you have any information on this woman's whereabouts, please contact the police at the Paris central prefecture.

Pierre turned away so that his dad couldn't see his face and smiled.

www.ingramcontent.com/pod-product-compliance
Lightning Source LLC
Chambersburg PA
CBHW070534130626
46555CB00003B/1410